KOZHUKATTA

PRONOUNCED KO-RRRU-KA-TTA

Sumi Chandrasekharan

Illustrated by Zafouko Yamamoto

tota books

tota books

KOZHUKATTA

Text Copyright © Sumi Chandrasekharan, 2017
Illustrations by Zafouko Yamamoto

First Indian Paperback Edition, 2017

ISBN: 978-81-762-1296-0

Published by **tota books**

An imprint of **FULL CIRCLE PUBLISHING**

J-40, Jorbagh Lane, New Delhi-110003

Tel: 011-24620063, 24621011

contact@fullcirclebooks.in • www.totabooks.in

Printed at NUTECH Print Services, Faridabad, INDIA

17/11/01/10/SCANSET/NU/NU/OP195

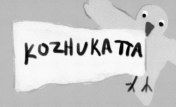

For my parents and my Ammumma, the storyteller -
I dedicate this to her memory.

Sumi Chandrasekharan

To all my friends who trust my cooking skills.

Zafouko Yamamoto

In a beautiful village in Kerala there lived a man called Ponnu who was very, very forgetful. He could remember almost nothing at all! This got him in a lot of trouble.

Sometimes he would go to brush his teeth...

...then forget, and eat a banana instead!

Then he would forget to peel the banana and eat it with the skin.

He would have a stomach ache and forget why.

All his wife could do was shake her head!

What bothered him the most was forgetting the names of all the wonderful things he ate. Ponnu loved food. He would say, "Janaki, can you please make, um...er...that thing for me that I ate the other day called, uh...mmm..."

Poor Ponnu! It was all very frustrating!

So on this fine morning, Ponnu rubbed his stomach and thought, "It's been so long since I saw my friend Kunju. Today is perfect to do just that!"

He said goodbye to his wife Janaki and set off.

"Good thing he can remember his way home, at least," she thought.

Kunju's arms were wide open for his friend when he arrived.

Ponnu sat waiting very still for Kunju while delicious sounds and smells filled the house.
"I can't wait to eat," thought Ponnu.

Out came Kunju and his wife from the kitchen with hot, frothy coffee and a tray full of goodies. There were crunchy snacks and munchy snacks, curly snacks and swirly snacks...

....and what were those?!

Ponnu had never quite seen them before!

"Hmm..." thought Ponnu blowing on a mysterious steaming hot dumpling before sinking his teeth into it. Mmm...I am floating on a white cloud of rice. The scent of coconut and spice is lifting me higher.

Delicious!

"WHAT IS THIS?"

"This? This is a Kozhukatta" said Kunju.

Kozhukatta- zh like rrr in purr. Say it purr-fectly.

  Soon after Ponnu finished the delicious snacks, he got up to leave. "If I don't start for home right away, I will surely forget this name just like all the others," he thought.

So he said, "I should leave now. Janaki will worry if I don't reach home before dark. Goodbye and thank you, especially for those delicious...um... what were they called again?"

He had already forgotten!
"Kozhukatta," Kunju reminded him.
"Yes, of course. Ko..zhu..ka..tta!"
repeated Ponnu.
"Oh how am I going to remember this?" he wondered.
"I know! I'll write it down!"
And he did. But...

Poor, poor Ponnu!

So...he bent...and he turned ...and he twisted himself, fowards... then backwards

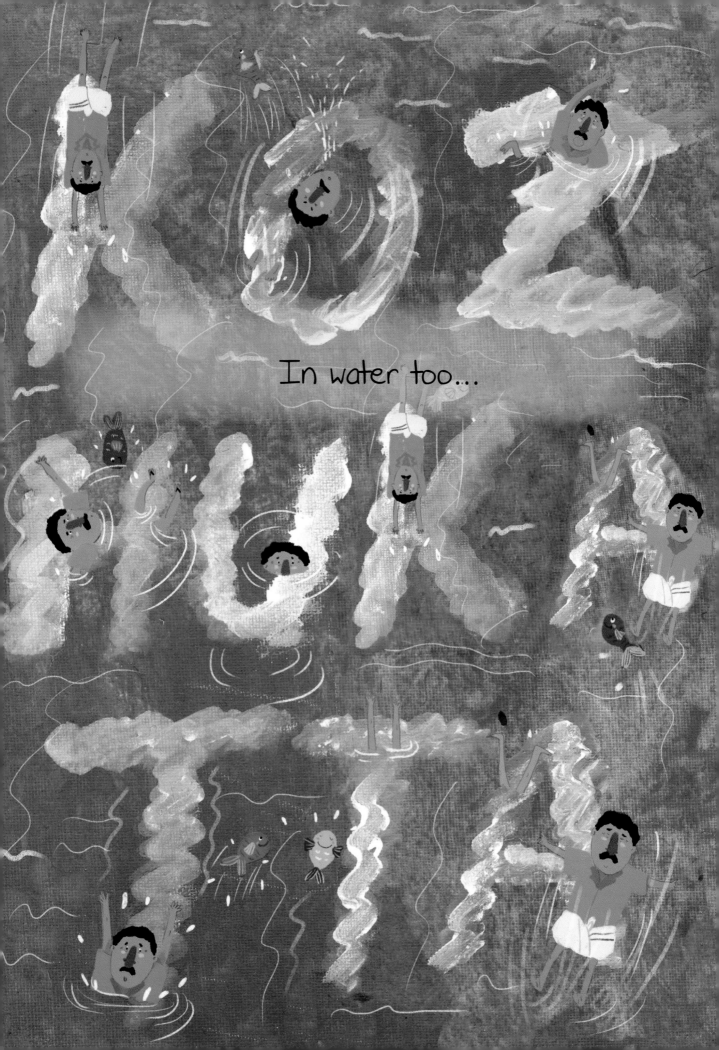

In water too...

Then chanted...

zhukattakozhukattakozhukattakozhukattakozhukattakozhukatta
Twenty five times uphill
kozhukattakozhukattakozhukattakozhukattakozhukattakozhukattakozhukatta
Ten times downhill

Over and over, he repeated the word, until he could

"I did it!" thought Ponnu as he saw the light from his house.

He did not forget! 'Kozhukatta' was still bobbing in his mouth and humming in his head. "Seven more steps and I'm home..."

He picked himself up, holding his aching head...but WAIT!!!

WHAT WAS THAT WORD!!!

"K-K-K-Kozhicurry?...
Kattukozhi?...
K-k-k? Cheh!
WHAT...WAS...THAT...WORD?
Somebody! Tell meeeee!"

JANAKIIIIIII!!! he wailed as
he ran the rest of the way home.
"Uh-oh! It sounds like my dearest
has forgotten something again,"
muttered Janaki, rolling her eyes.

"Do you know how to make er...um...k-k-?" he bumbled.
Poor Ponnu! He had tried really hard not to forget.
"Don't you know it, Janaki? Round, soft, white...and...nice?
Rossogulla?...Idli?"

And so he went to bed that night with a sad and achy head.
The next morning, Ponnu woke up, his head still throbbing.
Will he remember? Won't he remember?

"Aiyyyoooo!!!" cried Janaki.
"What is that on your forehead?"
"Oww," winced Ponnu, feeling
the lump from yesterday's bump.
"It looks like a...a..." stuttered Janaki.
"Like a what, Janaki?" asked Ponnu.

"A...a...KOZHUKATTA!!" gasped Janaki.

"That's it! THAT'S THE WORD!"

And so Ponnu remembered
the name of the delicious
dumplings he had eaten the
day before. And his wife knew just how
to prepare them for him, served with
hot and frothy coffee.

KOZHUKATTA

Glossary

Kozhukatta- steamed dumplings made from rice, coconut and spices.

Rassogolla- A round, white, spongy cottage cheese and semolina dumpling soaked in sugar syrup.

Perfect on a rainy day with tea!

Onion pakoda - Onion slices dipped in a batter of gram flour and deep fried crisp.

Idli- A round, white, soft steamed, cake made from a batter of fermented rice and lentils.

GulabJamun - A round, brown milk dumpling fried and soaked in rose flavoured Sugar syrup.

Samosa - Pyramid-shaped pastries stuffed with a mixed vegetable filling.